A NOTE ABOUT THE TEXT

The song we know today as "Over the River and Through the Wood" is adapted from a poem by Lydia Maria Child. The poem was first published in her popular three-volume anthology for boys and girls, *Flowers for Children* (1844–1846). During the nineteenth century it was reprinted many times under various titles. Child's poem became the unofficial anthem of Thanksgiving after her friend John Greenleaf Whittier included it in *Child Life* (1871), his immensely popular collection of nineteenth-century children's verse. The original poem was twelve verses long, but it has often been shortened to six. This book uses the six verses that appeared in the Whittier anthology under the title "Thanksgiving Day."

Illustrations copyright © 1993 by Christopher Manson

Published in the United States by North-South Books Inc., New York.

Library of Congress Cataloging-in-Publication Data is available.
ISBN 1-55858-210-X (TRADE EDITION)
ISBN 1-55858-211-8 (LIBRARY EDITION)

1 3 5 7 9 10 8 6 4 2
Printed in Belgium

The illustrations are woodcuts painted with watercolor
Musical arrangement and typesetting by Perry Iannone
The text and display type is set in Adobe Caslon
Typography by Marc Cheshire

Over the River and Through the Wood

A Thanksgiving Poem by Lydia Maria Child

ILLUSTRATED WITH WOODCUTS BY

Christopher Manson

North-South Books

NEW YORK

Over the river and through the wood,
To Grandfather's house we go;

The horse knows the way
To carry the sleigh
Through the white and drifted snow.

Over the river and through the wood—
Oh, how the wind does blow!

It stings the toes
And bites the nose,
As over the ground we go.

Over the river and through the wood,
To have a first-rate play.

Hear the bells ring,
"Ting-a-ling-ding!"
Hurrah for Thanksgiving Day!

Over the river and through the wood,
Trot fast, my dapple-gray!

Spring over the ground
Like a hunting hound!
For this is Thanksgiving Day.

Over the river and through the wood,
And straight through the barnyard gate.

We seem to go
Extremely slow—
It is so hard to wait!

Over the river and through the wood—
Now Grandmother's cap I spy!

Hurrah for the fun!
Is the pudding done?
Hurrah for the pumpkin pie!

Allegro

Lydia Maria Child

2. Over the river and through the wood,
   To have a first-rate play.
   Hear the bells ring, "Ting-a-ling-ding!"
   Hurrah for Thanksgiving Day!

   Over the river and through the wood,
   Trot fast, my dapple-gray!
   Spring over the ground Like a hunting hound!
   For this is Thanksgiving Day.

3. Over the river and through the wood,
   And straight through the barnyard gate.
   We seem to go— Extremely slow
   It is so hard to wait!

   Over the river and through the wood—
   Now Grandmother's cap I spy!
   Hurrah for the fun! Is the pudding done?
   Hurrah for the pumpkin pie!